DREAMS OF AN AMERICAN EXILE
Eric Z. Weintraub

ISBN-13: 978-0692521908
ISBN-10: 0692521909

Edited by Kimberly Sadler
Artwork by Ryan Sanchez

Printed in the U.S.A.

BLACK HILL PRESS
blackhillpress.com

Black Hill Press is a publishing collective founded on collaboration. Our growing family of writers and artists are dedicated to the novella—a distinctive, often overlooked literary form that offers the focus of a short story and the scope of a novel. We believe a great story is never defined by its length.

Our independent press produces uniquely curated collections of Contemporary American Novellas. We also celebrate innovative paperback projects with our Special Editions series. Books are available in both print and digital formats, online and in your local bookstore, library, museum, university gift shop, and selected specialty accounts. Discounts are available for book clubs and teachers.

Novellas

Special Editions

The Plaza Literary Prize is an international novella competition, organized by 1888 and Black Hill Press. The City of Orange, California was incorporated on April 6, 1888 under the general laws of the State of California. The center of the town became known as the Plaza, which has become a symbol of the community.

The Plaza Literary Prize celebrates the novella, a distinctive, often overlooked literary form that offers the focus of a short story and the scope of a novel. We believe a great story is never defined by its length and welcome all genres and themes with compelling characters and evocative moments. We're looking for our generation's Hemingway, Oates, or Steinbeck.

In America, she was Rose Quintero. She was the girl who majored in political science at the University of Arizona, the girl who would be the first person in her family to graduate college, the girl whose parents told her to bubble in "white" on her standardized tests' ethnicity questions. But she hadn't been that girl since the police arrested her. An unknown Mexican girl had replaced her.

She sat on an Immigration and Customs Enforcement bus that drove south on Interstate 10. Through the chain mesh and tinted windows, she saw downtown Tucson. The sun turned the glass walls of the One South Church building a blinding white. The windowpanes of the Bank of America Plaza reflected the blue sky. In the background towered the Santa Catalina Mountains where she'd grown up. She held back tears, so they wouldn't blur the last look at her home. She tried to put her hands up to the glass, but they'd shackled her wrists to a chain running to her ankles, and her ankles to the floor. After living in Eloy Detention Center for forty-five days, she thought of all the things she'd never experienced in Tucson. She'd never gone thrift shopping down Fourth

Avenue with her friends. She'd never hiked Sentinel Peak with her sister, so Jessica could paint the skyline. She'd never given her parents a tour of her college. She always had the same excuses: she needed to study, Sentinel Peak was too far by bus, she could go to Fourth Avenue any night. She'd lived in Tucson for twenty years. She never knew her life there had a time limit.

After merging onto Highway 19, the bus turned away from her home. The sprawling green pastures and distant mountain ranges of Cochise County entered her view. The bus drove down the highway to Nogales, a place her parents had told her never to go—a city across the border.

§

The bus parked under a white roof suspended above concrete beams that made the U.S./Mexico border-crossing look like a glorified gas station. The agent on the bus was dressed in a black ICE uniform. He walked down the center aisle, unlocking each deportee from their seat. The twenty people who crowded the bus had dark skin and brown eyes. The men's hair looked brittle from stress, the women's hair crusty from so many nights on a bullpen floor.

Before her arrest, Rose would've said she looked nothing like these people. She had light skin and green eyes. Her sun-kissed brown hair tumbled weightlessly over her shoulders. Her long, defined legs and toned upper body came from years of racing track and field. Only the curve of her inky black eyelashes revealed her Mexican heritage. But after being detained at Eloy, she felt humiliated to admit she looked exactly like them. Her hair clumped into knots. The rice and beans they fed her at the detention center made her stomach turn soft. Her body had the same sour dampness of skin covered by a bandage too long. The odor emanating from her white blouse and blue jeans revealed they hadn't been washed since her arrest.

Once the ICE agent uncuffed her, Rose rubbed her chaffed wrists and stepped off the bus. The distant stench of an open sewer made the city smell poor and dirty. Except for an hour a week in the exercise yard, she hadn't been outside since she arrived at Eloy. The wave of heat that now enfolded her like a blanket made her feel free. But as she followed the other deportees through a gate onto the Mexican side of the border, she felt she was stepping into a new kind of prison. Her professors used to lecture about the dangers of Mexican border towns: how drug cartels went to war over the best shipping routes, how shoot-outs occurred in broad daylight, how innocent people were raped and executed for sport. She hoped her professors meant cities like Juárez and Tijuana. Her friends used to come to Nogales on the weekends to drink; it couldn't be that dangerous.

She distracted herself with more positive thoughts. Here, no guards would watch over her. Nobody would tell her when to eat or use the bathroom. She'd have enough freedom to fix her immigration status and return home.

The moment she stepped foot on Mexican soil, a customs officer dressed in slacks and a polo waved her and the other deportees into a cube-shaped bungalow under the suspended roof. Inside the bungalow she passed from window station to window station where customs workers explained things in Spanish she couldn't understand, took down her information and handed over deportation papers that were shaped like her high school report cards. Her birth name, Rosa Quintero, sat on the front of the document. She hid it in her pocket before anyone noticed, fearing that once they saw she'd never go by her American name again.

Exiting the bungalow, no uniformed personnel stood to direct her. She had no idea where to go, so she followed the other deportees. They crossed the street and walked down a sidewalk below a highway underpass. The sidewalk curved around a dirt hill and rose up on an incline below a highway sign that read "BIENVENIDOS NOGALES SON" in a large white font. Ahead, fifty people stood in line outside a small shack guarded by a chain-link fence. The words "Centro de Atencion al Migrante Deportado – Nogales, Sonora" were stenciled on a low rising brick wall below the fence. Each person held their deportation papers. Their faded leather hats and dirty flannel jackets reminded Rose of the gardeners in her old neighborhood.

At the intersection where the sidewalk ended, Rose stood in the back of the line. She had no money and could only pray this center helped her find food and shelter. She didn't realize she was biting her nails until she tore the edges off of three. To concentrate her thoughts, she closed her eyes.

§

Since her arrest, Rose had spent every day in a bullpen so crowded with women that she only saw the floor when she looked at her feet. At night, everyone took turns sleeping because there wasn't enough space for all of them to lie down. She only left the bullpen when the guards escorted the women to the cafeteria. While eating rice and beans, she scanned the crowd for her parents' faces. The best part of her day came every time she realized ICE hadn't detained her parents and locked them inside with her.

After a week of staying strong, she begged the guards to let her go home. Every day, she stood at the bullpen entrance, looked them in the eye, and explained she was an American. She didn't belong here any more than their family members did. Only one guard listened to her story: a skinny, ex-Navy man who wore glasses with round frames. "ICE makes mistakes like this all the time," he said. He promised her as soon as he had the chance, he'd let her use a phone.

One night after lights out, the steel bullpen door slid open. A flashlight shined over the sleeping bodies of the women who shared Rose's cell and stopped once it found her face. The guard stepped over the women and offered his hand to help her up. Looking at him, she felt a love and respect she'd never felt for any other man. He was her hero, her savior, the most selfless person she'd ever met. She followed him down the hallways, quiet and empty this time of night, to a door he said was his office. Following him through the door, she didn't see a desk or a phone, only two guards waiting for them inside a cement-walled isolation room.

Rose felt so stunned she didn't move until the guard who promised to help her brandished his nightstick and struck her in the leg. Her knees buckled and the other guards caught her before she collapsed. She tried to jerk free, get her legs out from under her so she could kick, but the strength of two grown men left her powerless.

The guard who brought her pulled a handful of beer bottle caps from his pants pocket and lined the upturned caps in two rows on the floor. She stopped bucking. Her mind raced to find a way out before they hurt her more. They pushed her down to a kneeling position and the ridges of the upturned bottle caps sunk into her skin. For the next thirty minutes, they commanded, she needed to hold out her arms. If she dropped them, they'd make her start over. She tried to focus on her breathing, not the agony in her shoulders or the headache coming on from stress and exhaustion. She couldn't control the tears in her eyes, but she refused to break eye contact. As much as they tried, they would not break her.

"You're not an American," said the guard she had trusted. "My brother was an American. He was a soldier. He died for this country. And not just so you could come squat in it."

Her muscles felt so strained she imagined she looked like a bomb at the moment of exploding. She wanted to scream back at them, spit on their polished shoes, but the piercing pain of tissue ripping in her shoulders made her certain they were right. She didn't go to war for this country. She didn't contribute to American history. They made her believe she was just a miserable little girl who snuck over and pretended to belong.

By the time the punishment ended her arms felt so sore she couldn't raise them for two days. The bottle caps left deep gashes in her knees that looked like teeth marks. The rest of her time in Eloy she never spoke to another guard. She didn't see it as giving up, but as saving her breath, so that the day they released her she'd have the strength to get home.

Her third week inside, a lawyer came to her. Nobody from her family sent him, her case simply landed on his desk. They sat across from each other at a metal table in the empty cafeteria. He wore a beige suit, too big for his skinny shoulders.

"I want to help your family, Rosa, but your parents left a messy paper trail," he said, removing a stack of papers from his briefcase and placing them on the table. Rose looked through the pages: scanned images of her parents' Social Security cards, her dad's driver's license, her mom's green card. "Forged documents," the lawyer said, "all used to purchase property, get credit scores, open bank accounts." He spoke fast, as if he repeated these accusations to people like her fifty times a day. "I'm afraid these are grounds for deportation."

Rose's parents always told her their papers were only weeks from arriving. They'd forged documents so they could build a life in America while their files wound through the long immigration process. When they became legal, they planned to sell everything and start over as legitimate citizens.

Rose looked through the documents as if she might find a helpful answer. "We've lived here all my life," she said. "My parents brought me here when I was two—" She paused, believing that if she said anything else she'd only incriminate her mom and dad more.

"Your parents," the lawyer said, "were removed last week. They've been placed on a lifetime ban. They can never live in this country again."

Rose put her head in her hands, not wanting to hear another word. She wouldn't blame her parents if they disowned her after this. They had operated a chain of laundromats in Tucson. They owned a house in the suburbs. They were living the American dream and her arrest had snatched it away from them.

"There's two ways we can play this," the lawyer said. "Plead not guilty to living in this country undocumented and you'll spend the next twelve months awaiting trial. You lose that trial and you'll spend up to a year in prison before you're deported. But plead guilty now and you bypass that. Soon as a judge carries out the sentence, they'll release you into your birth country."

She lowered her hands. "And I'm on a lifetime ban, too?"

The lawyer gathered the papers back into his briefcase. "We couldn't find any falsified documents in your name," he said. Rose held her breath. Of course they hadn't, she thought. She'd destroyed those papers the moment she learned they were fake. "You're on a ten-year ban."

Ten years. The time she needed to get a doctorate from Georgetown. The time she'd given herself to work on election campaigns before she got a permanent job and settled down. The lawyer placed a plea bargain on the desk. She didn't want to go to Mexico, but she saw no other way out of Eloy, so she signed the paper.

The morning of her deportation, the guards allowed the women in her bullpen to say goodbye to their visiting families in the cafeteria. Rose wasn't surprised when no one came to see her. Her parents had been deported; her aunt and uncle who lived in Tucson were also undocumented. Only her sister could've come. Rose's mom was pregnant with Jessica when they crossed the border. Jessica was born in a Pima County hospital, and therefore, a legal U.S. citizen. But she feared her sister stayed home because she blamed Rose for everything.

§

Rose stood in line for two hours. By this time, the number of migrants had doubled. She hadn't eaten anything since Eloy served her rice for breakfast. An acidic swell of hunger rose in her throat. Almost ready to walk away, she noticed three women dressed in black and a priest wearing a clerical collar coming down the street to unlock the chain-link gate. The line of people began to enter the center. The three women greeted each deportee with a hug and checked the dates on their deportation papers. Because she did not speak Spanish, Rose feared the women would not take her seriously as a deportee. She knew a bit as a kid, but her parents stopped speaking it once they learned English. They said they had enough trouble being Mexican in a city like Tucson, they didn't need to advertise.

"Bienvenidos a El Comedor," one of the women said when Rose reached the gate. Up close, Rose noticed this woman wore a sweater in 100-degree heat. She had stringy hair and a large chin that accentuated her smile.

"English?" Rose said, trying to steady her voice.

The woman shouted to someone inside and a second woman dressed in black stepped out. She appeared younger than the other two, about the age of Rose's mom. Her nose looked thin enough to cut glass, her graying hair was pulled back tight into a bun and her tired face clashed with the youth in her large brown eyes. She led Rose down an unlit hallway into a kitchen just big enough to cram a refrigerator, stove and sink inside. Stainless steel vats on top of the stove bubbled, releasing steam into the air. The room felt humid and smelled like beans.

"Welcome to El Comedor," the woman said in such a thick accent Rose couldn't tell whether she spoke English or Spanish. "You are a college student?"

"Yes I am," Rose said, though she didn't know if that was still true. She'd been arrested before finishing her last semester of college. Her professors likely gave her zeros on her finals. U of A never asked for proof of citizenship before, but she wondered how she'd explain what happened when she returned to school.

The woman handed her one of the steel vats from the stove. "Carry this into the dining room. Start serving people." She plunged a ladle into the beans. "Later, I speak to you, I help you interview a deportee, whatever you like."

The woman thought she came to volunteer. Rose would've corrected her mistake if she hadn't felt so flattered she wanted to hug her. Rose's whole life everyone saw her as American, so when ICE threw her in with the Mexicans and the Guatemalans and the Hondurans, she forgot how it felt to have someone identify her the way she saw herself.

She carried the pinto beans into El Comedor's main hall. The inside of the shelter was no larger than a classroom and appeared as if the people who built it had no understanding of architecture. Tarps covered the roof where they'd ran out of sheet metal, steel beams supported the ceiling instead of walls and painted tapestries concealed the perimeter to hide the chain-link fence. On one tapestry, a hiker with a walking stick accepted food from the Virgin Mary. On another, dark-skinned women cloaked in white shawls held their babies. Standing beside a tapestry, the priest closed his eyes and led everyone in evening prayer.

Over 100 people sat squeezed beside each other at the long, metal tables. Rose stood on her toes, hoping to find her parents' faces in the crowd, but only the people from her bus looked familiar. She scooped beans from the vat onto plastic plates and passed the plates down the tables. Once the priest stopped praying, the people devoured the food. Rose wanted to serve a plate for herself, but had no time for a break. Before she even served others, a girl with a nose ring called for seconds. The woman from the kitchen brought her another plate and told Rose they served people until the food ran out.

"Their deportation papers are their tickets inside," the woman said. "We let them come in for fifteen days after they're deported. Two meals a day."

Rose had no idea how they fed so many deportees. So many people crowded into El Comedor: girls too young to have developed breasts, boys too young to travel alone, adults too old for manual labor, and more waited at the door. Everybody held the same deportation papers. Everybody had fifteen days before they had to decide where else to go. She wondered who would end up where. Some would go back to their homes south of the border. Others would return to the American city that deported them. In her poli-sci classes, she'd heard about those who tried to cross back, the ones who walked through the desert, ran out of water, and died.

She needed the fifteen days to figure out her own plan. She didn't think any of her family still lived in Caborca, the town where she'd been born. She had no idea whether the town was dangerous or what sorts of people she'd encounter on the journey there. Risking her life to cross the desert wasn't an option she imagined either. She didn't know what to do. She only knew she was hungry.

After passing out seconds, she stepped into the kitchen hallway and ate the last beans she could scrape from the vat. The food felt thick as mud sinking down her throat. The salty juice made her wince, but she drank it like broth.

"¡No!" The woman said from the kitchen doorway. She yanked the vat from Rose's grasp. "Son para los deportados."

Rose raised her hands. Her lips trembled because she couldn't remember whether I'm sorry was *lo siento, perdón,* or *discúlpeme.*

"Please. Wait." Rose fumbled through her pocket to find the deportation papers. "I didn't mean to trick you," she said, unfolding the creased pages. "I'm a deportee too."

The woman snatched the papers out of her hand to examine. She glanced at Rose like a cop determining whether to throw the suspect in jail. "No, I am sorry," she said, handing back the pages. "I should not have assumed." She shook Rose's hand with the stiff posture of a politician. "Mercedez de la Fuega Gúzman. Everybody calls me Sister Mercedez." Rose realized the women wore matching black clothes because they were nuns. All the outfit missed was an old-fashioned coif.

"Rose Quintero," she said. By giving her American name, Rose felt like she was lying again. Her last name sounded wrong coming out of her mouth as well. In Tucson, she always pronounced Quintero like the girl's name Quinn. After being surrounded by Latinas, her tongue had changed the sound to kin.

§

After dinner, the sisters who ran El Comedor lent the deportees old flip phones to call home. If somebody's family didn't answer, they handed the phone to the next person in line. Rose thought of so many people to call for help: her professors from school, her teammates from track, but she'd never memorized anybody's number besides her sister's. Once she received the phone, she faced a corner where two tapestries met and dialed Jessica's number. With each passing ring, she had less and less hope.

—

12

On the fourth ring, her sister answered. "Hello?"

Rose held the phone closer. "Jessica, it's—"

"I'm sorry, I can't answer the phone right now." Jessica's voicemail stopped to giggle. "Please leave me a message."

Rose didn't move, not only because she didn't want the nuns to realize the call didn't go through, but because she didn't want to believe her sister ignored her. Whether Jessica was at dinner, in class or watching a movie, she always answered her phone. Now Rose would have to wait till tomorrow to call again. Jessica couldn't help her cross back, but she could at least come down here, help her feel less afraid.

Rose whispered into the phone so no one but Jessica heard her voice trembling. "I'm in Nogales—I'm on the other side of the border. I don't know what to do, Jess. It's getting dark outside, I don't even know where to sleep tonight." She put her hand over her eyes. "I need you to come down here tomorrow. I need you to bring money, clothes, anything you can carry and meet me at the crossing terminal." The nun tapped her shoulder. "I'll wait there all day for you."

She thought to end the message with "I love you." She never said the words enough when they lived together, but now things had changed. Tragic situations were supposed to push people together. But she didn't want to say I love you, not to a machine. She'd save it for when her sister arrived.

She closed the phone and handed it to the next deportee.

§

"We run a shelter nearby," Sister Mercedez told Rose after a majority of the deportees left El Comedor, "but I'm afraid we don't have space tonight." Instead, the sister helped her by asking a family of three, two brothers and a wife, to guide her to a different shelter. When they left El Comedor, the sun had set behind the hill on the far side of the street. Only the dark haze of blue dusk hung over the night sky. Another highway sign hung over the road above El Comedor. It read "FRONTERA USA" and pointed downward, back toward the border. She felt like Mexico had placed it there on purpose to taunt her and every other deportee.

The family didn't speak to her. They huddled together and walked down Calle Reforma, a narrow two-lane road with few streetlights. She walked, looking at her feet, careful not to trip over wide cracks in the asphalt. They walked past houses and storefronts with bars on the blackened windows. Every house was painted a different bright or pastel color. The only sound came from sneakers kicking a plastic ball down the road. Ahead, a group of boys played soccer, passing the ball around a darkened Ferris wheel in an empty lot. Nogales felt like a city forgotten by the people who created it. It was nothing more than a way station between Mexico and America. Nobody wanted to fix it because everybody was passing through.

The whole time they walked, she thought of home. Tucson was only seventy miles north. If she could sneak across the border and find a bus, she'd be standing on her front porch in an hour. She missed the most basic things: sleeping in her bed, waking up spiraled in the sheets, showering in private, cooking her own meals. But if getting home was that easy, places like El Comedor wouldn't exist.

After half an hour, they hit the first intersection on a major city street. Here, the road ran parallel with the border wall. She hated the look of the wall's towering, eroded steel. It not only barred her from her homeland, but the gap between each brown beam taunted her, just wide enough for her to reach her arm back onto American soil. Ahead, a massive two-story crossing terminal branched over the wall. Its beige paint and tinted windows reminded her of an airport. A freestanding white roof in front of the terminal arched over both vehicle checkpoint directions like a dove's wings ready to take flight. While cars and buses rushed south down the highway, vehicles waiting to go north inched forward in permanent gridlock. Rose believed that when Jessica arrived she'd likely come through this crossing station, not the one where ICE deported her.

After so many days in detention the city's fast pace made her feel like a wild animal that wandered into civilization for the first time. They walked past food stands serving customers, billboards hanging from three-story buildings to advertise mariachi bands and shops carrying merchandise for tourists, like ponchos and sombreros, that played raggaeton on their radios. Not even downtown Tucson got this busy at night. The blaring sounds and colorful lights felt like a way to distract tourists from the real Nogales.

They walked south, leaving the city center behind. She followed the family off the highway, down a road flanked by tall white walls that blocked her vision of the neighborhood. They stopped walking when they reached a small church made of beige bricks. The oldest brother knocked on the polished wooden door.

"Ya no hay más cupo," a woman said from beyond the door. The brother yelled back and knocked harder. The woman didn't honor him with a reply.

After having no luck with five more shelters, they trudged exhausted and thirsty back down Calle Reforma.

15

The family led her off the street through a bent-open metal gate into what she thought was a vacant lot.

When her eyes adjusted to the dark, she realized she was standing in a cemetery. The cemetery curved up on a hill covered in wooden crosses that marked the names of the deceased in white chalk. So many headstones and mausoleums crowded the hill that it appeared difficult to walk between the graves. The cemetery wasn't perfectly manicured like ones in the U.S. It looked dirty and menacing, as if people only tended to it when someone needed to be buried.

The family sat in a circle behind a brick mausoleum. As if on cue, the temperature dropped. Rose's arms shook. The sound of voices coming from deeper within the cemetery made her ears perk. She wanted to go back to El Comedor, look for the sisters' shelter. But the oldest brother turned his back on her, letting her know she was no longer their responsibility. She could go back alone, but people more dangerous than the boys playing soccer might now lurk in the streets.

With no other option, she hiked up the wooden steps at the center of the cemetery to find somewhere hidden to sleep. Every sound made her muscles constrict. She feared someone might lunge at her from behind a tomb, wrap their clammy hands around her body, and drag her into the shadows. The sight of other migrants sleeping here made her flinch. Their heads rested against crosses. Their bodies were covered with filthy blankets. She saw teenagers playing cards, a woman rocking her crying baby to sleep, an obese man holding a forty-ounce in one hand smiled at her through a drunken haze. She couldn't believe this world existed so close to her home. She couldn't believe she'd been born in this country.

Near the peak, she found a solitary grave plot. It looked safe, hidden behind a mausoleum and enclosed by a thin steel gate. The name Jose M. Chavez was written on the black cross in white chalk. Only one date marked the gravestone: January 31, 1980. She didn't know if this was his birth date or death date.

She lay on the plot, trying to make herself look invisible. But she didn't know how to sleep fearing someone might sneak up on her. What would happen if she died in Nogales? There would be nobody to tell the graveyard workers her birthday. Her family and friends would never even know where she was buried. She felt as helpless as the afternoon of her arrest, on May 14th, forty-five days ago.

§

She'd attended a rally to protest the state's decision to close a dozen schools after the budget shortfalls. As a favor to Robert, a friend from her comparative politics class who helped organize the rally, she stood on the sidewalk in front of City Hall taking pictures of the other protestors. Each protestor carried a sign with a different message written in marker like "Save Our Schools" and "What About Our Futures?"

Someone must've complained to the police because an hour into the protest, a squad car arrived and told them to disperse. Robert screamed back at the officers, accusing them of persecuting his free speech. He was heated, the way he often got during class discussions. When the officers stepped out of the car, he picked up a large rock from a lawn of dead grass and threw it at them. The rock sailed across the sky, spinning on its heavy path through the wind. It flew so close to Rose's face she could've reached out and caught it. Instead, it smashed a spiderweb-shaped crack into the windshield of the police car.

After that, things happened fast. The officers drew their guns. Everyone got on the ground. Back up arrived. They were all arrested. When an officer booked her in the busy police station, he announced something was wrong. There were Rosa Quinteros in the system, hundreds of them, but not her. As far as America was concerned, Rosa Quintero did not exist outside her school records. She knew this, of course. She'd known she was undocumented since she turned eighteen. Through college, she'd kept a low profile, never joining any political clubs or participating in any government internships no matter how good they stood to look on an academic résumé. She thought there'd be no harm in attending a rally. She now realized she had been careless.

§

Lying in the cemetery, Rose looked out at the few houses in Nogales with lights on. She wished her parents were here to protect her. Where were they sleeping tonight? Far away from a cemetery, she hoped. Safe inside a shelter, lying in a small bed, her dad holding her mom close. If she could get through the night, she'd go to the American consulate tomorrow. She'd find a way to convince them her family deserved visas.

Rose rolled onto her side. She used her arms as a pillow and apologized to Jose M. Chavez for sleeping on his grave. Throughout the night, the throbbing of her exhausted brain never tucked away under the blanket of sleep. Her eyes closed and her thoughts turned to abstracts, but she shot awake at the sound of any cough or snore and jumped at the tingle of a bug on her arm.

Hours from sunrise, a girl's scream made her eyes shoot open. Not a loud scream of warning, but a muffled scream of helplessness. A high-pitched squeal followed by a moan silenced by a hand. A quieter noise replaced it, the squishy sound of wet skin rubbing in the night.

Rose scrambled to hide behind the mausoleum. She shut her eyes so they didn't reflect moonlight and held her breath so nobody could hear her. Somewhere down in the dark cemetery, a girl was getting raped. She thought of the deportee she'd followed around the city. The woman who rocked her crying baby to sleep. Her own mother. She wanted to help, but if the rapist carried a weapon, she'd be the next victim.

She could only listen to the girl's moans, Rose's beating heart the one part of her body left unparalyzed. Her face strained to hold back tears. What right did she have to cry? She thought she lost every shred of dignity when they deported her. But she was wrong. Listening to someone in pain, doing nothing to help, made her feel she'd sunk to a deeper low.

"Stop," the girl said between grunts. "That fucking burns."

The girl's English jump-started Rose. She had to act. She needed a weapon. Gulping down a hot breath of air to steady her nerves, she stood up, hugged the gate, and swung her legs out of the plot. Dirt piles of the recently buried covered graves nearby. She searched the graveyard, hoping a digger left out a shovel. It was so dark she kept crouched, careful not to fall inside an open tomb. She found candles and flowers among the graves, but nothing she could use as a weapon.

Fearing more rapists lurked below, she dashed up the hill. At the peak, a chain-link fence divided the cemetery from the street above. She crawled through a hole in the fence and snuck to a row of parked cars. Streetlights cast a sodium-vapor glow over the road. As if it might help avoid detection, Rose covered her face with her hair. She checked the cars, hoping to find a baseball bat or crowbar in a backseat. Every time she released a locked handle, it slammed back into the door as loud as her pulse drummed in her ears. At any moment an owner might come out and catch her, but she tried every car. All the doors were locked. Only a paint bucket in a truck bed came close to a weapon. It wasn't ideal, but she had no time.

She crept down the hill crouched between the tombstones. With every step, the sound of wet skin grew louder. Something squishy she stepped in made her slip and crash paint bucket first into a grave marker. She scooted backwards to hide in the shadow of a mausoleum. Someone heard her, she knew it. She only prayed they didn't come looking.

She wished her dad were here—her mom, her sister. But she was alone. Below, the rapist tortured the girl. There was no time for self-pity. She pushed herself up and continued down the hill.

Sound guided her. Inside a mausoleum no larger than her family's backyard shed, she found them. Moonlight shot through a window on the far wall, silhouetting their figures. The rapist held the girl trapped beneath his body and above a stone tomb. His pants around his ankles, he rammed his skinny waist into her from behind, licked the back of her neck and grunted like he was about to come. The girl's eyes stayed shut. Tears ran down her cheeks.

Rose steadied her arm. She took a deep breath and rushed into the mausoleum. Arching the paint bucket over her shoulder, she hurled the blunt force onto the rapist's head. His teeth cracked together, his eyes squeezed shut. He lurched off the tomb and knocked over a painting of the Virgin Mary on the wall.

"Run," Rose said. "Hurry. Go."

The girl looked back at Rose in terror, as if she was a second attacker rather than a savior. The rapist—who she thought she knocked out—cursed in Spanish and scrambled to close his pants. Rose jumped back out of the mausoleum. She expected him to charge at her, wrestle her to the ground, but he only stared at her like a hungry dog that had its dinner taken away.

"What the fuck is your problem?" the girl said. Rose thought she was talking to the rapist, until she hiked up her pants and kissed him on the cheek. "¿Carlos, estás bien?"

When the girl's face hit the moonlight, Rose recognized her from El Comedor. She had a piercing through her left nostril, black hair that covered one eye, thick glasses and a round body that looked frumpy dressed in a man's wife beater. She had asked Rose for seconds before others got firsts.

Rose feared she'd misinterpreted things. The rapist hadn't dragged the girl here; she'd come of her own free will. Maybe he was her boyfriend. This mausoleum was the only place they could go for privacy. But if that were the case, why was he hurting her?

"¡Vete!" The man screamed in the girl's face. "Puta desgraciada."

The girl picked up her backpack and darted for the exit. She spat at Rose's feet and pushed her aside. Rose shook with too much panic to register the insult. The rapist still stared at her, working to memorize her face. Without hesitation, she dashed back into the cemetery to hide. She knew she could outrun him. She could outrun most people in Arizona.

§

In El Comedor's single stall bathroom, Rose brushed the rancid morning breath from her mouth. She almost didn't recognize herself in the mirror. Her reflection looked dark and ugly. Bags sagged under her eyes from staying awake all night. Her fingernails were filled with dirt and her neck leaned crooked from sleeping on the ground. If she hadn't been so hungry, she would've skipped breakfast and gone straight to the consulate. But she needed all her energy. She believed today would be one of the most important days of her life.

She walked into the main dining room. Sister Mercedez pointed to an empty seat next to where she served breakfast. Rose thought to ask if she could help pass out food again — she didn't want Mercedez to see her like the other deportees — but she was in a rush and needed to eat fast. She sat down and Sister Mercedez served her a plastic bowl of oatmeal from a vat. After so many days of eating rice and beans, the oatmeal tasted as delicious as pancakes.

"I am sorry again about the confusion yesterday," Sister Mercedez said. "I did not realize you are a Dreamer."

Rose looked up from her bowl. "A what?"

"A Dreamer." Sister Mercedez served oatmeal to another migrant. "An undocumented child who thinks they're American. You don't know the word?"

Rose had heard the word. She'd seen it around school, hung from thumbtacks on hallway notice boards, printed onto pamphlets on professors' office doors. "DREAMers" were undocumented children who might one day go to college and gain citizenship. She never identified as one—not with her parents assuring her they were almost residents. She wanted to correct Sister Mercedez, but she liked the nun's definition. The name stood for her old life. She would do anything to experience that dream again.

"No, I know the word," Rose said.

Sister Mercedez nodded, glad that was cleared up. "You see her?" She pointed to a girl sitting two tables down, the one Rose saved last night. "The girl with the—¿cómo se dice?—nose ring? Her name is Claudia. She's a Dreamer too, from Phoenix. You should talk to her."

Claudia met Rose's stare, then looked away without acknowledgment.

"I should," Rose said.

With the deportees' plates full, Sister Mercedez excused herself to carry the serving vat back into the kitchen. Rose continued eating while stealing glances at Claudia. Claudia was not the kind of person she would talk to in America. She reminded her of what most Latinas in her high school had been like—the ones who dismissed college as something only meant for rich white kids, the ones who now worked at fast food restaurants and already had two babies.

Rose looked down at her oatmeal. She used to think she was so much better than them. Neither of them had anything over the other anymore. She wanted to meet Claudia. She could use a friend here, especially a Dreamer.

She grabbed her bowl and walked two tables down. "I'm Rose," she said, extending her hand. Claudia kept her eyes on her bowl. Rose could tell she wasn't welcome, but sat down anyway.

"Who said you could sit here?"

"I was only trying to help you last night."

"Did it look like I needed help?"

"It looked like you were getting raped."

Claudia's eyebrows raised above the rim of her glasses. "How long were you watching us?"

Rose couldn't believe she'd risked her life for this kind of thank you. She scooted in closer. "You were crying."

Claudia ate a spoonful of oatmeal. She looked surprised Rose hadn't left. "Why are you still here?"

"Sister Mercedez told me you're from Phoenix—"

"So?"

"So, I just got deported from Tucson. We're in the same situation. I thought we could help each other."

"We are not in the same situation. I never asked for your help and I never asked for you to sit down. Fuck off."

Claudia catapulted oatmeal off her spoon, making Rose jump up to dodge it. The food landed in a pasty clump on the concrete floor. Rose thought of so many nasty things to say to Claudia, but she kept her mouth shut. She didn't want Sister Mercedez to feel like she'd contributed to this senseless drama. Like Claudia did last night, Rose left without saying a word.

§

South of the main crossing terminal on a street that ran parallel with Highway 15, Rose waited in a long line outside the U.S. consulate. She stood at the back of the line, beyond the cement awning that hung from the beige building to provide shade. The sun burned her neck. The back of her shirt dripped with sweat. While everyone else in line wore suits and dresses, she now wore clothes El Comedor had given her: cargo pants, a wrinkled "I Love New York" t-shirt and a green backpack covered in blotchy yellow stains. She'd thrown away her old shirt and jeans, parting with the few possessions she had left from Tucson. She hoped her appearance helped her case.

After an hour, she entered the consulate. The air conditioning cascaded over her body, sending a shiver down her spine. She took a number from the security table and sat on one of the red benches. In the consulate waiting room, people crowded the rows of seats. Most sat in silence. Two women ran rosary beads through their fingers. Only families made noise, the parents bribing their kids with chocolates and picture books to keep quiet. Rose imagined every person in this room had a better chance of getting to the United States than her. They didn't come to beg, but to pick up their first green cards, renew their old visas. She prayed her consulate worker would take pity on her and help.

After her number was called, she sat in a chair on one side of a dividing station that cut the room in half to separate the employees from the immigrants. The nameplate of the consulate worker who sat across from her read: Daniella Contreras. Daniella looked ten years older than Rose. Her body was soft from sitting at a desk for so many years. Damp, black hair draped past her bony shoulders. So much green eyeshadow covered her eyelids that Rose could see the brushstrokes.

"¿Cómo te llamas?" Daniella said.

"Rosa Quintero." She always gave her real name to authority, but now wondered if her American name would've better helped her cause.

"¿En qué le puedo ayudar?"

"English, please?"

"How can I help you?"

Rose placed her hands on the edge of the desk like a politician giving a speech. She explained she'd lived in Tucson her whole life, knew no other home and because she was almost ready to graduate college, she deserved a visa that would allow her to return to America. The way Daniella nodded, never interrupting, made her believe they could've been friends. After Rose finished her story, Daniella looked over her deportation papers and checked her file on a computer beside the desk.

Rose didn't want to breathe, for fear one small change in the air could ruin everything. She closed her eyes and the consulate grew quieter. Every baby stopped crying. Every person stopped breathing. She could hear nothing but Daniella's fingers moving across the keyboard.

"I'm sorry," Daniella said. "There's nothing I can do for you."

Rose hid the disappointment on her face. She figured the consulate wouldn't hand over a visa so easily. "Explain something to me. People get visas all the time. Why can't I appeal this?"

"You got deported. Didn't your lawyer explain that?" Daniella now talked with the same forced sympathy as the lawyer from Eloy. Rose didn't think this consulate worker saw her as a person, just as another number she'd called to her station.

"My lawyer threatened me with jail time. I signed a plea bargain under emotional duress. Don't tell me you can't help me."

"Hire another lawyer."

"With what money?"

"Miss, I am sorry." Daniella held up her hands. "There is nothing we can do for you here. If you don't mind, you have a lot of people waiting behind you."

Rose rubbed her stiff neck. Her throat felt sore. How was it she'd won trophies for her high school's debate team, but couldn't get this woman to meet her halfway? Daniella's mind seemed made up before Rose even sat down.

"My parents got deported," Rose said, lying back in her seat. "Do you have any idea how I can find them?"

Daniella put her hands on the keyboard. "What are their names?"

"Armando and Evelyn Quintero." She provided her parents' birth country and birth dates. As Daniella searched for her parents, Rose kept her face blank. She refused to give Daniella the satisfaction of disappointing her twice.

"Appears they were processed through Nogales a week ago."

Rose leaned forward. "Does it say if they came through this office?"

Daniella shook her head. "You can check with security at the front, but I don't know how that'll help you."

"Maybe they would've told someone where they were staying."

"Maybe." Daniella nodded, anxious to get her to leave.

Or where they were going, Rose thought. Perhaps her parents did go to Caborca. They'd grown up there. They met and married there. But the town was 100 miles south of here and she had no money to go look for them on a hunch. If she left Nogales, Jessica would never find her either.

Rose mumbled a thank you and stood up to talk to security. Daniella called the next number.

§

Rose found no trace of her parents by looking through signatures in the security's sign-in book. She left the consulate and crossed Highway 15, past the long line of cars waiting to enter America. The city center still moved with last night's pulse. Families filtered through the turnstile gates of the main crossing terminal, teenagers dashed down the street to catch the bus and vendors cooked *tortas de milanesa* in their portable carts. Now the smell of fried sandwiches made her stomach go cold. She had no money for lunch. If she wanted to eat in the next few hours, she needed to beg for change.

She stood in front of the wall on Internacional Street, at the street corner opposite the turnstiles. Every time she glanced at the border she felt a sharp pain, like someone pricking her heart with a tiny needle. As people passed, she measured up whom to ask. She didn't think Mexicans returning home would give her money, but hoped an American tourist would take pity on her if one walked through. The idea of approaching anyone humiliated her. In America, people begged her for change. What if one of her old classmates saw her? She could already picture them laughing about it in Tucson. *Remember Rose?* they'd say. *That girl who was too busy studying to ever hang out? Guess where she is now...*

As the hour dragged on, she determined less Americans came to Mexico these days. A city where migrants got raped in the cemetery was not the ideal getaway. But hunger kept her from giving up and in the early afternoon two Americans crossed through.

"Excuse me," she said to the middle-aged couple dressed in jeans and matching blue shirts. "These two men jumped me last night. They took everything. My wallet, my passport...can you please help me? Even just a dollar."

The husband looked over his shoulder like he thought she was scamming him. "Why don't you go to the consulate?"

"I waited there all day. Please, I'm starving."

The wife nudged her husband. "Don't be cheap. Give the girl some money."

The husband sighed, but handed Rose two dollars from his wallet. With the crisp green bills in her hands, she held back tears. The two dollars made her feel rich. She could buy lunch. She could make a phone call. Anything seemed possible. She wanted to hug the couple. She said, "Thank you."

They wished her luck and walked away holding hands. Rose envied them. If life were a lottery, the winners were born in America. Anyone who knew her never would've guessed she was illegal. She'd grown up in one of the nicest suburbs in Tucson. She'd planned to take a year off after graduating to work and save up money for grad school. By her twenty-fourth birthday, she wanted to be working toward her Masters in political science. At twenty-six, complete her thesis on the future of Millennials in conservative politics. At thirty, balance work with starting a family. At thirty-three, get a doctorate. At fifty, become a senator. Somewhere along that timeline, she'd imagined, she'd earn her green card and citizenship like her parents had promised.

Now, none of that would happen. Her dreams were snatched away in an afternoon. Her unfinished college education counted for nothing. Here she was a blank slate, a bum who didn't exist unless someone stood right in front of her, an unknown Mexican girl people took pity on until they walked away. She feared that one day she'd remember her life in the U.S. as nothing more than an extended vacation. She could learn Mexico's political system and pursue a career in her birth country, but who would vote for a middle-class immigrant turned homeless deportee?

§

She'd learned the truth four years ago, before her first semester of college. She'd wanted to live in a dorm, but her parents told her to commute. There was no reason to spend all that money, they said, when she only lived fifteen minutes from school. Instead, she asked if they would pay for her driver's license.

"You don't need a license," her mom said one afternoon when they went grocery shopping. "You can take the bus."

"My last class doesn't end till seven. I don't want to take the bus that late."

This conversation went on for weeks. When she got an idea in her head, nobody could change her mind. She saved up the money her parents gave her for helping clean the laundromats in order to pay for the driver's license herself. On the car ride home from her cousin Isabella's first communion, she told her parents the plan. It was 1:00 a.m., her parents were both a little drunk from the celebration, and she believed they'd be more accepting in their good moods. She wanted them to see she'd taken the initiative, that she could be business-minded like them.

"I saved up the money," she announced, sitting in the backseat next to Jessica, who slept with her head against the window. "And I'm going to the DMV on Monday." Her parents both sat silent. Her dad turned off the radio and her mom said something in Spanish. They spoke Spanish so rarely Rose forgot they knew it. She prepared to argue against any reasons they gave her.

"You can't get your license," her mom said.

"I'm eighteen. I can do what I want. Dad, why aren't you on my side about this?"

Her dad said something in Spanish that made her mom's eyes turn alert and sober. "Armando…" her mom cautioned.

"You don't have a Social Security card," her dad said.

"Yes, I do," Rose said. "It's in my closet."

"It's a fake."

Rose stuttered out a couple nonsensical words. She hadn't rehearsed for this kind of argument and almost believed her dad until she remembered how much he drank tonight.

She leaned toward her mom so fast the seatbelt locked on her shoulder. "What's he talking about?"

Her mom shut her eyes. "There's something we haven't told you."

Her dad looked at Jessica before keeping his eyes on the road. "Rose, you were born in Caborca."

She had no idea what they were talking about. They might as well have told her she was born a boy. "Caborca?" She laughed. "Where Grandpa lived?"

Her dad glanced at her in the rearview mirror and told her the story. She wasn't born in the hospital on Grant Road, but in her grandparents' house in Caborca. For the first two years of her life, they lived in the house while her dad worked at a gas station down the street. Around the time her mom became pregnant with Jessica, he got laid off and couldn't find stable work. They barely had enough money to put food on the table, they never could've afforded a second child. With no time to wait for a visa, they left for the U.S. in search of a better life. They took a bus to Tijuana and crossed through an underground tunnel to enter California. Her mom had to crawl inside the tunnel while eight months pregnant with Jessica. Her dad carried Rose harnessed to his back.

Every time her dad glanced at her, she felt she was supposed to give some kind of dramatic reaction. But she couldn't connect the places and events to her own life. She'd gone to school with the American kids. She'd been a Girl Scout with the American girls. A different birth country didn't change the fact that she was still an American. Looking out the car window, she half expected not to see her own reflection. But the washed-out shape of her face floating in the black night looked back at her. She was still here. She was still the same person.

Once her dad finished speaking, the car was so quiet Rose could hear the tires drive over the pavement markers. "Why didn't you tell me before?" Rose said.

"It's nothing to worry about." Her dad nodded his head with every word. "We've waited years for our papers. We'll be residents soon."

"But if I went to the DMV and they realized I was illegal, they'd deport me."

"Not necessarily." This time he didn't look in the mirror. "I'm sorry. We never told you because we didn't want to scare you."

Rose wanted to forgive him, but she didn't feel like she knew her parents anymore. They were always smart, cautious people—yet they risked arrest, deportation, and death just so they could own a business and a home. Her whole life they'd lied to her.

"You're driving a car. Or is your license a fake, too?"

"Rose, please," her mom said. "We'll talk about this tomorrow. Armando, get us home. I'm exhausted." The car went quiet. Her dad kept the radio off.

Once they got home, Rose ran to her room. She tore up her fake Social Security card, her fake birth certificate, anything forged she could find that would get her into legal trouble if she were caught. After the papers lay shredded in the trash, she went to bed hoping she might somehow solve this problem when she woke. But the next morning she only had a moment of peace before last night's memories came rushing back. As the days went on, the information sunk in. She felt forced to question everything she knew about her life and how this problem would affect her future. She stayed home less, spending fifteen hours a week in the library studying for her AP exams. She tried to distract herself from the constant paranoia that if her parents got caught she'd be sent back to a home she never knew.

Entering college, she thought of switching majors. An undocumented girl studying political science made as much sense as a blind person going to film school. But she decided the best way to cope with her new circumstances was to continue life as normal. She'd gained an interest in politics by watching the news to prepare for debate competitions.

Every time she saw a woman take the Senate floor, speak with the perfect composure she tried to mimic, she thought, why couldn't she be one of them? Declaring a different major would mean not living up to her full potential. And didn't her parents risk everything so she could realize her dream? She'd so far lasted her whole life in Tucson. Being made self-aware didn't make her any more likely to get deported.

Even now, she couldn't believe she got sent back. She couldn't believe she was sitting on a bus bench, eating an apple and a bag of corn tortillas bought with money she begged for, looking through the wall for any sign of her sister. She wondered how Jessica was getting by alone on the other side. Their parents had always granted her sister special privileges, never making her work at the laundromats or do chores. She got to focus on her one true passion: painting. Growing up, Rose thought their parents coddled Jessica because she was the baby of the family. But no, it was because Jessica was the American. Jessica even had the middle name Esperanza, Spanish for "hope." She was their parents' blessing, their American dream. Rose had no middle name.

§

Her second night in Nogales, Rose found a place to sleep at Amistad Cristiana de la Frontera, the shelter that denied her access the first night. She showered off crusty grime from sleeping in the cemetery all night and dried sweat from standing in the sun all day. Fewer deportees stayed in this shelter, but migrants as young as five had come here from all over the continent: Guatemala, Honduras, El Salvador, and those were just the ones she recognized. They looked even more desperate than her. Their lips were cracked open from the sun. Their faces were bruised from being beaten on the way to the border. Some had bandaged stumps where their legs and arms should have been.

Rose walked down the hallways and through the shelter's church hoping to find her parents. But the only person she recognized in the shelter was Claudia. Claudia sat on a corduroy couch in the center of the shelter's community room. Claudia looked at her. Rose nodded back, half showing she still acknowledged her, half hoping the gesture pissed her off.

That night she slept in the bottom bunk bed farthest from Claudia in a room filled with twenty other women. Just one day without a bed had made her exhausted, but she couldn't sleep. It wasn't the women's snores that kept her awake or the moans some girls made. It was the distant sound of gunfire that grew louder and crept closer throughout the night. Rose thought of the migrants from the cemetery who didn't have the luxury of a shelter to protect them. Somewhere out there among the muzzle flashes and executions the rapist roamed the city, praying on other girls, searching for her, so that he might get his revenge the best way he knew how. She didn't like looking out the window. The shelter kept it open because it was so hot inside. Every time she glanced at it, she thought she'd see him standing outside, watching her, crawling through the opening.

When the rising sun turned the sky a blazing orange, Rose gave up trying to sleep. She stepped into the empty hallway and sat on a bench outside the door. Though the lights in the community room were on down the hall, she didn't hear anyone talking. Only the hum of the fluorescents kept her company. She couldn't remember the last time she had privacy. She felt so exhausted, even more frustrated with her inability to sleep. Her head was heavy, her skin greasy with night sweat. She wanted to crawl out of her body and stay that way. Now felt like a good chance to cry. Before she released her tears, the bedroom door opened. Claudia stepped into the hallway.

"You can't sleep either?"

Speaking even a syllable would make Rose's voice crack. She stood up and walked toward the community room.

"I'm sorry I yelled at you yesterday," Claudia said. "I get it, you were just trying to help. But that guy in the cemetery? He wasn't raping me."

Rose turned around and took a labored breath. "You said, 'That fucking burns.'"

"It hurt like hell, but I wasn't getting raped. He's a coyote. Said if I fucked him, he'd charge me less."

"So you weren't getting raped, you were being exploited."

Claudia pointed a finger at Rose. "Don't judge me."

"Would it have killed you to tell me this earlier?"

"I didn't know who you were. Sister Mercedez told me what happened to you…" She threw her arms open like she wanted to hug Rose, but felt too embarrassed. "I only came out here to say I was sorry."

She appeared less threatening in the hallway's even light. Her skin still looked clean from last night's shower. The way her sweaty ponytail draped to one side reminded Rose of college girls who dashed to their 8:00 a.m. classes without time to dry their hair.

"I forgive you," Rose said. She crossed her arms. "How'd you find a coyote?"

"Looking to get your cherry popped?"

"Shut up." Rose laughed, blinking the last tear from her eyes. "I'm just asking."

"So you're looking to cross?" Claudia put her hands on her hips. "I've tried crossing four times."

"Is it as bad as everyone says it is?"

"It's like a passage out of Exodus. Endless days in 100-degree heat. No shade. Except instead of Egyptians, you're running from *la migra*." Claudia sat on the bench, leaving enough space for Rose to join. "They don't just deport you either. They stick you in Eloy for a couple weeks first."

"I've been there too." She sat beside Claudia.

"No one ever told me it's a felony to get caught crossing more than once. Right before they deported me the second time, they hit me with the lifetime ban. No shot at ever being American again." Claudia rubbed her shoulder and laughed like the joke was on her. Rose almost reached out to comfort her, then remembered how Claudia had treated her yesterday. "I'm meeting with this new coyote next week to see if he can help me," Claudia said. "You can come with if you want. Least I can do after you saved me from being" — Claudia nudged Rose's ribs — "exploited."

"I'm not gonna fuck anyone," Rose said.

"It might help you relax."

"You're such a bitch."

"I'm a bitch?" Claudia hit her own chest. "If you just waited five seconds he would've finished."

The thought of hiring a coyote tempted Rose. She could escape Nogales, be with her sister in Tucson, and find a way to go back to school. But the police already caught her in America once. If border patrol captured her again, they'd put her on a lifetime ban, too. She'd lost everything when she got deported. She didn't know if she could risk losing her last chance for a future in the U.S.

"I better sleep on it," Rose said.

"Just let me know by the end of the week. He's got a good deal. He'd probably let us both cross for 15,000 pesos."

She remembered hearing ten pesos equaled one dollar. "What is that, 1,500 U.S.? That's not a good deal."

"You kidding? It's a steal for a coyote. I hear he charges less 'cause he makes you carry drugs. He's connected with the cartel."

The same fear Rose felt when she entered Nogales crept back into her chest. The feeling that the cartel lurked just around the corner and she had no choice but to face them.

"How do you know he's safe?"

"A lot of guys in El Comedor have taken him before. You'd know that if you spoke any Spanish." Claudia rocked back and forth on the bench. "You want to get breakfast? It's early enough, I could be first in line for once."

Now that Claudia spoke to her, the day seemed less lonely. She imagined they could be somewhere else. They weren't getting ready to go to El Comedor, but off to enter a dining hall at U of A.

Rose nodded. "I'll grab my shoes."

§

Rose and Claudia walked west on Internacional Street. The sun peeked over the hilltops east of the city center, illuminating the shops that had not yet opened.

"Did you go to college?" Rose said.

"Never got around to it." Claudia lit a cigarette she took from behind her ear. "My ma worked at ASU though. One of those women who delivers the right Bunsen burner to the right chemistry class."

"Why didn't you go there?"

Claudia blew smoke away from Rose and didn't answer her question.

Where Internacional Street curved to meet Calle Reforma, thirty people stood in a circle outside an auto repair garage. They wore jeans and grimy t-shirts covered in a week's worth of sweat. Through the gaps in their legs, Rose saw a man on the ground. Blood dried into the asphalt below his head. A ratty blanket covered his body. On the far side of the circle, a police car sat stalled while an officer unrolled *precaucion* tape around a fence post and a street sign.

"Can you believe this?" Rose said.

Claudia walked around the circle. "He was on the street at night. What did he expect?"

Rose couldn't look away. She'd never seen a dead body, never even been to a viewing. The way the body lay perfectly still under the blanket didn't seem natural. The chest arched out like the man was ready to sit up, but couldn't, like he'd fought for survival till the blood ran out. This could easily be her, Rose thought. In a couple days her time in Amistad Cristiana would expire. If she couldn't find another shelter, she'd be out on the street again. Ten-year ban, lifetime ban — the consequences she'd face returning to the U.S. felt insignificant compared to her fear of winding up a corpse in the street.

She looked up at clear sky on the other side of the border. The desert crossing didn't sound so much like suicide anymore. The Sonoran may be perilous, but so was Nogales. She'd gladly trade ten years of danger for a three-day hike. Unlike most migrants, she had an advantage. She knew the landscape. She'd spent more hours than she could remember riding buses to track meets in Ajo or Yuma staring out at the rocky terrain that streaked by outside her window. The desert was enormous, but with the help of a coyote they wouldn't get lost. Most of the desert was covered in trees and hills, plenty of spots to hide from border patrol. When they stopped walking, they could rest in the shade. They'd survive.

Rose caught up to Claudia. "When did you say you're meeting the coyote?"

§

After breakfast, Claudia invited Rose to hustle money with her. She followed Claudia behind El Comedor where they filled water into a bucket hidden in the weeds. Together, they walked to Highway 15. Claudia offered to wash people's car windshields while they waited in traffic for the crossing checkpoint. Most drivers said no, some gave her the finger, but every ten cars or so let her wash their windshield for twenty pesos. She cleaned the windshields before the car pulled forward and dried the glass spotless before the sun left water splotches.

Rose watched from the center island between the two directions of the highway. She stood on the only manicured lawn she'd ever seen in Nogales and leaned against a white pole beneath the Mexican flag.

"Rose." In front of a minivan, Claudia waved her over. "I wash, you dry. Let's go."

Rose didn't move. Begging for change yesterday embarrassed her enough, she couldn't become one of those homeless people who approached cars, spray bottle and rag in hand. She glanced at the wall to see if her sister was standing there, if her sister could see her.

Claudia dried the minivan's windshield and stepped onto the island. "What's wrong with you? You sick?"

"I don't want to get in your way."

Claudia pulled a handful of pesos from her pocket. "You can make some real money doing this. But I'm not splitting anything unless you dry."

"I'm sorry." Rose bit her lower lip and pointed at the cars. "I've only been here three days, everything is so sudden. This is so weird for me."

Claudia stepped back. "You may've been Mexican in America, but here you're about the whitest girl I know. You don't want to do some shitty job 'cause you're afraid some stranger will look down on you? That's your decision. But you'll never afford a coyote."

Claudia turned away and scanned the line for another customer. Rose didn't have a comeback because Claudia was right. She didn't mean to sound like a princess, it just came out that way. She'd gone to college because she didn't want to perform manual labor in her parents' laundromats anymore. She didn't want to perform manual labor anymore because it reminded her she was undocumented. Once she got home, she hoped she would never have to work in the sun again. Right now, she had no choice.

Claudia waved down a pick-up truck that looked like it had rammed grill first into a swamp of mud. Rose took the drying rag from Claudia's hand and followed her. For the next three hours, Claudia washed and Rose dried. They only cleaned four cars, but the extreme heat and increasing hunger made Rose grow dizzy.

During a lull in traffic, they rested beneath the flagpole. Claudia pulled a plastic bag filled with jalapeños out of her backpack and offered some to Rose.

"It's too hot for something that spicy." Rose pushed back the food. "But thanks."

"They're not spicy." Claudia's teeth crunched into the chili's smooth green skin. "They'll fill you up."

Rose knew she couldn't spend any money on lunch, not if she expected to raise 15,000 pesos, so she bit into the chili. At first it tasted like a green bell pepper, then grew hotter. She swallowed it before it burned her mouth and sucked in air to cool her tongue.

"Homeland Security made a mistake," Claudia said. "There is no way you're Mexican." Claudia pointed a chili at her. "Rose. That even your real name?"

Rose ate the next jalapeño out of defiance. "If you must know, it's Rosa."

"I like that. Rosa…" Claudia rolled her R's to speak the name. "It's got a better ring to it."

"It made me stand out in Tucson."

"Suits you better here. I'm calling you Rosa for now on."

For a moment, they both sat, too tired to talk. She felt Claudia knew almost everything about her, but she knew almost nothing about Claudia.

"How'd you get deported?" Rose said.

Claudia stopped chewing the jalapeño. "When I was eighteen, me and my ma moved back to Tuxtla Gutiérrez. It's the capital of Chiapas. Know where that is?"

"In the south of Mexico." Rose felt too embarrassed to admit she only knew this because her cleaning lady was from Chiapas.

"She got cancer. That's why we went there, so she could die. She had a lot of family in Tuxtla—not to mention my older brother she left behind." More cars drove past but neither of them moved. "For a while, we thought she'd pull through. Lots of herbs, lots of church. Then we ran out of money for the meds."

"Aren't drugs dirt cheap here?"

"For you rich girls, maybe. Can't make much when your family works off the land." Claudia brushed hair out of her eyes. "I planned to move back to Phoenix, send her money from there. But by the time we figured it all out, my visa expired. The print shop where I worked wouldn't sponsor me. I couldn't take a plane. I've been trying to cross back since."

"How old are you?"

"Twenty-one."

Claudia's life in Phoenix ended only three years ago, yet Rose thought she looked twenty-seven, maybe thirty. She wondered if the struggle of living in Mexico sped up people's aging. She'd been so focused on getting home, she never stopped to think what would happen if she got stuck here another three years. At what point did Claudia's desperation to cross outweigh pride? At one point did she give her body to a coyote?

"Is your mom still there?" Rose asked.

Claudia tossed a jalapeño stem on the ground. "Didn't find out she died till I made a phone call from Eloy."

"I'm so sorry." Rose scooted closer to her. "You don't want to go back to Tuxtla?"

"What for? She wanted me to live in the U.S. I'm gonna finish what I started."

"Where's your dad?"

Claudia shrugged. She turned the last jalapeño in her fingers like a diamond. "I left Tuxtla eighteen months ago. I think I've eaten more jalapeños on this journey than some Mexicans have picked. They're the perfect travel food. Small, but filling. One day, all food's gonna be just like this."

Rose didn't want to imagine how many days Claudia survived off chilies alone. Before now, she'd never gone hungry. She never knew how it felt, how she could think about nothing without food in her stomach. But the jalapeños did help her feel full, at least to last her until El Comedor.

Claudia ate the last jalapeño and stood up. "*Vámonos*, Rosa. Let's do a couple more cars."

§

The next four days, Rose and Claudia worked on Highway 15. By cleaning together, they washed double the windshields and split the profits. The more sunburned Rose got, and the greasier her hair became, the more money tourists gave her. Their third day, they made almost 200 pesos between them. She worked with Claudia for five hours before splitting up in the afternoon to wait for her sister at the border wall. She didn't feel comfortable staying at the wall for more than an hour. Men her father's age whistled at her, shouting "Chupa me la" as they passed. Sales girls mistook her for a tourist and tried luring her into their stores to buy prescription drugs. Car mufflers backfired on Highway 15 making her dive under a bus bench fearing she'd heard a gunshot.

Every day, she grew more restless. She stared at the cement parking lot on the American side of the border with her head pressed against the wall beams. She didn't know why she thought of them as beams. They were bars. Mexico was a prison that kept her from her homeland, from her sister, from the future she worked so hard to build. She hated the wall. She hated it the way she hated Robert for throwing that rock, the lawyer for sending her here and her sister for never showing up.

At night, she sat across from Claudia at a table in El Comedor. Sweat from the day's work covered their bodies. The pesos they'd collected sat in their pockets. Claudia always closed her eyes for evening prayer while Rose sat wishing her parents brought her up to be religious. Death would seem less terrifying if she could look forward to an afterlife. She tried not to think about the man in the road, how his family probably comforted each other by saying, he's in Heaven now. She wanted to believe that too, but from a young age she'd felt certain that only the mind generated consciousness. Once it shut down, a person went blank like they never existed. She supposed these thoughts kept her moving. She needed to either escape or face an eternity of emptiness.

Rose shook off the thought and they talked about what they missed most in America. Claudia missed going to the farmer's market every weekend to pick out fresh fruit with her mom. She missed getting drunk at her friends' houses and wandering out for fast food at 2:00 a.m.

"Know the first thing I'm gonna do when I get back to America? Go to a bar like a normal twenty-one-year-old."

"You'll still need a fake I.D.," Rose said.

"Fucking shut up."

Rose missed the simple things. She missed going to a cold movie theater on a hot day. She missed taking a shower after a three-mile run.

§

Today was the Fourth of July. From the other side of the wall the aroma of barbequed meat wafted through the air. East of Highway 15, Rose and Claudia walked past fireworks vendors who stood on the street corners, on their way to meet the coyote. They turned down an alley off Avenue Ruiz Cortinez Eje onto a back street. The street didn't look menacing as Rose expected, but residential. Lemon trees lined the paved road to provide shade. Colorful *papel picados* hung from string lines that extended across the street.

They stepped through a door beneath a second-story balcony into a dimly lit restaurant. In the courtyard behind the restaurant, the coyote sat alone at a circular table drinking a beer. His face lingered half in the sun, half in the shade of a stone column that supported the roof. He had a purple-dyed mohawk and the same caramel-colored skin as Rose's dad. His sunglasses and heavy stubble covered any other distinguishable facial features. She didn't like the idea of going into the desert with this man. His appearance, everything from his sense of style to the way he crossed his legs, made her think he was hiding something. She glanced to see if he had a gun.

"¡Buenos días! Me llamo Sol." He stood up to shake their hands and motioned for them to sit.

Once Rose and Claudia introduced themselves, Claudia and Sol negotiated in Spanish. Rose couldn't translate in her head. She waited for Claudia to stop and interpret, but Claudia looked too focused to bother.

After what felt like half an hour of talking, Claudia said, "Está bien." She put her hand on Rose's shoulder. "Sol needs 500 pesos each from us."

Rose zipped open the backpack in her lap. "That's it?"

"That's the deposit."

"How much is he charging us?"

"20,000 each."

Rose closed her backpack. "You told me 15,000 for both."

"I told you it wasn't cheap." Claudia counted out the correct number of pesos from a plastic bag in her lap.

Rose looked down at the bag of coins in her backpack. In the five days she'd spent with Claudia, they'd made less than 1,200 pesos between them. At this rate, it'd take almost a year to afford a coyote. In less than seven days, they'd have to start paying for their own food and shelter. She worried Claudia had other ideas for getting a discount.

She leaned toward Claudia. "How are we supposed to make 39,000 more pesos?"

"Don't worry," Claudia whispered into Rose's ear. "I've done this before."

"How?"

"If all else fails? Steal it." Claudia looked past Rose like she was confessing an embarrassing secret. If Rose weren't so determined to get home, she might've told Claudia she was going too far.

"Perdón," Rose said to Sol. "¿Hablas inglés?"

"Do we have a problem?" Sol said. His English sounded proper, British dialect with a Mexican accent.

"We can't pay you when we get to Arizona?"

"When you get to Arizona, you'll be in the middle of the desert. You will pay the morning we go or you won't go."

"You want us to carry drugs, right?"

Claudia sighed. "Don't fuck this up again."

Rose raised her finger to stay quiet. "You'll make more money off the drugs than us. Why charge us at all?"

"You're older than most clients."

"What does that mean?" Rose said. She feared what not wearing sunscreen all week had done to her face.

Sol put up his hands. "Please understand. Usually, we have kids carry the drugs. The United States is much nicer to children. They don't get into as much trouble as adults do. But if you get caught, you face consequences—I'm talking about jail time—and that's bad for business. To avoid that, I need to be more careful when I help you cross. That's why I charge more." Sol raised his beer to his mouth, but stopped before drinking. "If I did not charge you, that would mean I did not value your life. I am not like the other guides. I won't leave you to die of thirst. I don't take you 200 miles west into the high desert." He put the bottle back on the table. "No, we go east, through Cochise County. I know every border patrol tower and sand drag between here and Tucson and I guarantee safe passage."

Rose nodded. Cochise was southeast of Tucson. She last passed through it when ICE drove her here. The landscape looked grassy, the mountains provided shade. Thanks to the monsoon season, Cochise stayed cloudy this time of year. She didn't know if she could trust the coyote. But she believed he had no good reason to abandon her. She'd be carrying his shipment and he'd take great care to keep her from falling into the border patrol's grasp. If a better option existed, she didn't see it.

"Okay," Rose said, "we'll go with you." She counted out 500 pesos from her backpack and placed them on the table. Sol slid the coins toward him and dropped them into a bag she hadn't noticed in his lap.

"On the eleventh," Sol said, "we meet at Panteón Reforma, the cemetery on Calle Reforma. You know where that is?" Rose and Claudia both nodded. The eleventh was

Rose's fifteenth, and last, day at El Comedor—Claudia couldn't have found a coyote with better timing. "Be there at dawn. It will take all morning to drive to where the Americans stopped building the wall. There we enter the desert. Beyond that, it's a three-day walk to Duquesne Road, where my partner will meet us and drive us to Tucson."

§

That same day their weeklong limit at Amistad Cristiana expired. Sister Mercedez helped Rose and Claudia find beds in the Nazareth House, the shelter she ran with the Comedor sisters.

"We only take women and children," Sister Mercedez said while giving them a brief tour. Unlike Amistad Cristiana, the Nazareth was a home rather than a church. It had private showers, a kitchen, and a telephone where deportees could call their families. Rose called Jessica again, but this time her sister's number was disconnected. She now felt too nervous to be angry with Jessica. She pictured Jessica in her same situation: sleeping in a tunnel under the freeway, begging for food on Congress Street, showing up filthy to class in the fall because she had no place to shower. But at least in Tucson Jessica knew people who could take care of her.

That night, Rose lay on one of the ten cots with the covers off. Her stomach growled and her chest felt empty. She tried to tune out the snores of the other women who crowded the room. Soon the sun would rise and she'd spend another exhausting morning washing too few windows for too little money. She wished she could have a day off just to sleep and eat. How was she supposed to face the desert when she already felt so exhausted?

A flash exploded outside the window, jarring Rose from her thoughts. The sound barrier cracked. Light burst past her peripheral vision and she jumped out of bed to hide on the floor. The next gunshot, she feared, would rip through her stomach. Her heart rammed against her chest like it wanted to tear through her skin and run off without her. Too paralyzed to sprint for the door, she curled into a ball, shut her eyes, and mumbled a prayer she didn't know.

She couldn't get killed. Not in the shelter. Not in the one place she felt safe.

The shots kept firing. Faster now. Faster than any one man could pull a trigger. She needed to get away from the window. Escape. She crawled onto her hands and opened her eyes, but looking up she wasn't met with the mass panic in the room she expected. A supernatural green light bathed the walls. It washed over the bodies of sleeping women. Only one other sat up in bed. Before the light faded, she realized it was Claudia. Claudia lay catty-corner to her, clutching her blanket, wiping tears from her eyes. She looked so vulnerable with her face puffy and her hair tied back, Rose felt like she'd never met the real Claudia until now.

Another shot fired and this time, the walls turned blue. Rose realized she wasn't hiding from gunshots, but fireworks. She peeked over her bed to see an orb of blue sparks explode in the night sky. How could she confuse the two?

She dropped down below the bed unable to look at the fireworks anymore. Her family always spent Fourth of July in Oro Valley. They picnicked on top of dense Mexican blankets and ate ham-and-cheese sandwiches in a field populated by a hundred other families who waited for the sky to get dark enough so the fireworks show could begin.

At this very moment, those families sat there watching fireworks just like these. She was sure none of them noticed that, for the first time in twenty years, her family was missing.

Claudia climbed out of bed and stood over Rose. "You fall out?"

"I guess so," Rose said, rubbing her head.

"Get up, stupid ass." Claudia offered her hand and helped Rose back into bed. She crawled under the covers with Rose and spooned her from behind. The feeling of Claudia's heart beating against her shoulder made her feel safe. She imagined she was being held by her mother or her sister.

"I want to go home," Rose said. She pulled Claudia's arm tighter around her waist. "Will the crossing really only take three days?"

"If Sol doesn't get lost." Claudia spoke like she was halfway inside a dream.

Rose glanced over her shoulder. "Did you ever have a coyote get lost?"

Claudia's cheek nodded yes against Rose's back. Questions now popped into Rose's head she never thought to ask before. Claudia survived four times—what about the people who crossed with her? If they got deported too, where were they? Why wasn't she helping them find a coyote? She didn't want to stir up any painful memories, but they were going into the desert soon. She needed answers.

"Did you ever see anyone die out there?" Rose said.

Claudia didn't answer. She was already asleep.

§

The next day, Rose and Claudia washed more car windows. Once the afternoon heat spiked to an unbearable temperature, they sat on the center island and counted the forty pesos they'd earned. "This isn't enough," Claudia said. "We should go to a pawn shop. Check out what they're looking to buy, so we can steal it from someone this weekend."

Rose took her half of the pesos, not trusting Claudia with her money. "I'm not gonna mug anyone."

"Then while I'm at the pawn shop," Claudia said, tossing a rag at Rose, "you wash. I'll meet you at the shelter." She stood up and crossed the highway back to the city center.

Rose looked at the rag covered in dirt and the wings of dead bugs. The thought of washing one more car in this heat gave her a headache. Instead, she went to beg for money at the turnstiles. She watched Mexican families filter through, carrying their duffle bags and wrangling their children. After an hour with no luck, she heard a familiar voice.

"Rose! Rose!"

The voice sounded so distant, she almost thought it came from her head. Beyond the wall, a woman sprinted toward her through the parking lot. Her skin was golden and her hair freshly washed. She wore a blue shirt, white jeans, and a red backpack that had once belonged to Rose. For a moment, she thought she was seeing her past self. She almost didn't recognize her own sister.

Rose dashed to the wall and threw her arms between the bars to hug Jessica. Jessica's hands felt warm wrapped around her sides. Her sister's hair smelled like Rose's old shampoo. If the space between the bars were a centimeter wider, their foreheads could've touched. She never should've doubted Jessica would come to the border. She felt a bond between them that had been absent before.

"I brought everything you asked," Jessica said. She took off Rose's old college backpack and tried to hand it through the wall.

"The turnstiles are right there." Rose's whole body shook. "Cross over."

For the next ten minutes, she waited outside the turnstiles for Jessica to enter. Seeing her sister step from one side of the wall to the other felt like an illusion. Something Rose wanted to do so badly, her sister performed with no effort.

Jessica clutched her hands against her chest. She had tears in her eyes. "You have no idea how relieved I am to see you, that you're okay..." They hugged again, this time wrapping their arms around each other's backs. "I have three hours till the last bus home. Can I get you lunch?"

They walked south down a pedestrian street lined with pharmacies and clothing stores. Her sister traveled so far, Rose wished she could treat her to a nice restaurant, but they ended up sitting on stools at the counter of a small food shack where she'd seen Americans eat after giving her money. The only light came from the open storefront entrance. The smell of roasted chicken covered Rose's sweaty odor.

After the cashier took their orders, Rose couldn't contain her questions. "So what's going on? Are you okay? Where are our parents? Where are you staying?"

Jessica held out her hands. "You do know the bank took back the house."

"I don't know anything."

The cashier interrupted, placing a diet soda Jessica had ordered on the counter. Jessica sipped from the straw inside the can. Her eyes moved back and forth like she needed to assess the right words. "The government froze everything. Now they're gonna sue Mom and Dad over the mountain of forged documents they created."

Rose wanted to say something optimistic, fulfill her older sister duties, but no words of comfort came to mind. The lawyer never indicated things would go this far. Their house was gone. Life as she knew it was over. It'd been over since Robert threw a rock at that police car. She just hadn't realized it till now.

Rose brushed hair out of Jessica's eyes. "Where've you been living?"

"With Aunt Esmy and Uncle Genaro."

Rose exhaled. "All this time, I kept picturing you on the street."

"Where are you living?" Jessica said.

"In a shelter."

Jessica held Rose's hand. "And you worried I was homeless?"

"Your phone was disconnected."

"The bank accounts were on hold. I couldn't pay the phone bill."

"So how'd you get my message?"

"I started working for Aunt Esmy. She's paying for my phone."

The cashier placed a burrito in front of Jessica and a chicken breast in front of Rose. Jessica swiveled on her stool to face the food, but looked at Rose before picking it up. "I didn't mean to make you worry. I would've come down here sooner, but it took a few days to get the passport." Jessica sunk her teeth into the burrito.

As empty as Rose's stomach felt, she had too many questions to bother eating. "I guess you haven't heard from Mom and Dad?"

"They haven't talked to you?" Jessica said with a mouthful of bean and tortilla.

Every nerve in Rose's body stood at attention. "No."

"They've been trying to get in touch with you for weeks."

"Where are they?"

"In Caborca."

Rose closed her eyes. "Why would they go back to Caborca? We don't have family there. All our grandparents are dead."

"They're living with Uncle Reyes."

"Who?"

Jessica sipped her drink. "One of Mom's brothers."

Rose massaged her temples as if it might help the information sink in. Now she knew her parents weren't far. She could take a bus, be with them by sundown.

"How'd you talk to them?" Rose said.

"They called Genaro."

"Do you have their number?"

Jessica looked over her shoulder and reached for an envelope in the backpack she'd brought. "The address and number's inside. The number's for our uncle's market though, so no guarantee they'll pick up." Rose opened the seal to notice a stack of twenty-dollar bills inside. Before Rose could ask, Jessica said, "It's about $300. Enough for you to go to Caborca—plus extra for Mom and Dad."

Before her deportation, Rose never would've imagined Jessica helping her this way. Jessica had never worked. She'd barely completed her community service hours to graduate high school. But in less than two months, she'd grown up. She looked older, provided for her family and even wore Rose's clothes. Rose felt less afraid knowing her sister could fend for herself.

"Do they want us to go to Caborca?"

"They asked me to stay in Tucson," Jessica said.

Rose understood. Her parents wouldn't want Jessica living in Mexico. They saw her as their American dream. Now she was the only part of the dream they had left.

"Thank you," Rose said, tucking the envelope inside her backpack. "So you're okay? Everything's okay? What about school? How did last semester go?"

Jessica looked down at her burrito like she didn't have the strength to eat another bite. "I dropped out of school."

"Jess..." Nobody, including Rose, believed Jessica would ever graduate college. But Rose had hoped that by getting her degree she would've set a good example. "You're supposed to transfer next year."

"You're seriously the last person who should be giving advice."

Rose hit her hand on the counter. "This isn't my fault. My friend threw a rock at a cop car."

"What were you thinking going to a political protest?"

Rose looked down at her food. "You're just upset."

Jessica sat crooked on her seat like she might jump up and leave. "If I'm upset, it's because you ruined my life."

"Don't be so dramatic."

Jessica counted off the bad things in her life on one hand. "I lost my parents. I lost my house. I lost all the shit inside my house. I lost any chance of ever living a normal life again. Now I'm living with a family that reminds me every day they're doing me a favor and a bunch of cousins who've turned knocking over my paint canvases into some kind of game. You put me in this position, so don't make me out to be this fucking slacker when I say I dropped out of school."

Rose grabbed Jessica's shaking hand and held it steady to calm her. "I understand," Rose said. "And I agree, it's all my fault. But Jess" — Rose swept her hand out toward their view of the street — "do you see where I am? I spend my days washing car windows for change. I couldn't even afford lunch before you showed up today. My first night here, I slept in a cemetery. I fought off a coyote with a paint bucket because I thought he was trying to rape someone."

"You're serious?" Jessica said.

Rose squeezed Jessica's hand tighter. "I'm sorry this happened to our family. Every day I've been here, I've thought about how hard this has to be on all of you. But Jess, you're the only one in our family who has a way out of this. You still live in Tucson. You need to keep moving forward."

Rose put her hands back in her lap. Jessica looked at her like she could picture everything. "I'm sorry I yelled at you," Jessica said.

§

Rose waited with Jessica for an hour in the pedestrian line to cross back. Reaching the terminal building, they hugged each other goodbye.

"I love you," Rose said. "Even if you hate me, I love you."

"I love you too." Jessica kissed her cheek. "There's nothing you can do to change that."

Rose stepped out of line, crouching under a guardrail to enter the street. Walking away, she looked back at her sister. She tried to remember every detail of Jessica: the way the light turned her brown hair blonde in the sun, the way stress formed crow's feet around her eyes to make her look like an adult, the way her skin burned where she forgot to put on sunscreen. Rose didn't want to stop looking. If she didn't make it to Tucson, she didn't know when she'd see her sister again.

She sprinted down Calle Reforma, eager to call her parents. When she entered the Nazareth House, Claudia wasn't back yet. She stood in a line of five people who waited to use the living room phone. Her leg shook and she felt light-headed. She glanced at the soccer match playing on the shelter's TV to calm herself, but the kids shouting at the game only made her head throb harder. How would her parents react to her voice? Would they hold her responsible for their deportation too? Would they plead for her to come live with them in Caborca?

After the woman in front of her finished talking, Rose sat in the wooden chair next to the desk. She picked up the phone and dialed her parents' number from the envelope.

On the second ring, a man answered. "Buenas tardes." Deep and guttural, it was the unmistakable sound of her dad's voice. She didn't want to speak for fear she'd never hear him again.

"Dad." She steadied her breath. "It's Rose."

For a moment her father stayed silent. Then he said, "Rose!" He called in Spanish for someone else to come to the phone. She pictured her parents in Uncle Reyes's market: her dad clean shaven again after being released from Eloy, dressed in one of the short sleeved button-ups he wore to combat the desert heat, scratching his milk-white sideburns while he waited for his wife; her mom getting back into shape after surviving the diet of rice and beans, her hair tied in a bun to stay cool, long-delayed stress lines developing on her olive-skinned face.

"Rose?" her mom said from the line. "Jessica found you."

"She did. I'm in Nogales."

Her mom shouted words of joy and thanked God in Spanish.

"I just wanted to let you know I'm safe," Rose said. She tried to keep smiling, but her voice caught in her throat. "Mom, Dad, I'm so sorry." She cringed through the next words. "Can you forgive me?"

"We put you in this position a long time ago," her dad said. "None of this is your fault."

Rose pulled the phone from her ear. She closed her eyes and stopped her leg from shaking. She wondered how she'd ever doubted they'd forgive her in the first place.

"Do you have money?" her mom said.

"Jessica gave me a little."

"Buy a bus ticket and come to us."

Rose didn't speak. She pictured herself living in her uncle's house, sleeping with her parents nearby to protect her, eating dinner at a table with family again.

"Evelyn," her dad said, "is that such a good idea?"

"She has nowhere else to go," her mom said.

The words made Rose sit up. Images of a life in Caborca left her thoughts. "What happened?"

On the TV, the center-forward sprinted toward the goalpost. All the kids stood and screamed at the game. Rose plugged one ear and pressed the phone against the other, not wanting to miss a word.

"We don't want to scare you," her mom said.

"I have to tell her," her dad said. "She has to be prepared."

The player made the shot. The kids screamed, "Gol!" Rose turned her head away.

"We saw people get robbed on the bus down here," her dad said. "Now we're paying taxes to the cartel just to live in your cousin's house. Rose, we know this isn't safe, but neither is Nogales and we want you to be with us."

Rose didn't know what to say. She wished she could go to Caborca and protect her parents. Even if they didn't blame her, she still held herself responsible for putting them in danger. But if she went to them, she'd only be a burden. She believed she could help them better from the U.S. She could hire a new lawyer, get a job under the table, and send them money to pay the cartel. She looked around the room and half expected the kids to be watching her now, judging her for planning to abandon her parents in Mexico. But she still had a chance to get home. She could rebuild her life in the U.S. That's what her parents wanted for Jessica, did they not want that for her, too?

Something brushed her shoulder, making her flinch. She looked up to see Claudia standing over her and jerked away before Claudia could ask who was on the phone.

"Do you know how to get to the bus station?" her dad said. She wanted to tell them her plan, get their blessing even, but she knew they wouldn't sleep for days waiting to hear whether she made a successful crossing.

"I'm sorry," Rose said. "They're telling me to get off the phone. I have to go."

"Are you in a shelter?" her mom said. Her voice sounded 1,000 miles away. Rose wondered how far it would sound when she called them from Tucson.

"I am. I'm sorry. I have to go. I love you."

"Just be careful," her dad said.

"We love you too," her mom said. "We'll see you soon."

Rose tried to memorize the sound of their voices, but didn't feel she deserved any more of their time. She took the phone from her ear and hung up.

"Who was that?" Claudia said.

Rose turned in her seat to look up. Her whole body shook. A cold empty feeling lingered in her chest. "I need money. We need to pay the coyote. We need to cross."

"Let's wait till Friday—"

"—it's our only way out—"

"Wait till Friday," Claudia said, massaging Rose's shoulders. "We'll rob somebody and get everything we need."

Rose's voice quivered. She nodded. She never felt so much like she'd met Claudia for a reason until now. Claudia would guide her through the desert. Claudia would get her home to Tucson. She'd never have her old life back, but she thought of how much she'd accomplished before her deportation and how much she'd still accomplish. She'd find a way to finish college. She'd make up for all she took from her family. One day she'd speak to her parents and they'd understand why she chose to cross.

Her face contorted and she buried her head into Claudia's shirt so Claudia couldn't see her tears. The tighter Claudia held her, the harder she cried.

§

On Friday night, Rose and Claudia sat against the wall of a gas station convenience store beneath a highway overpass a mile south of the border. Claudia smoked a cigarette while they looked at cars pulling in to fill their tanks. They both eyed possessions inside the cars they could lunge for and steal. Golf clubs lay in the bed of a truck. Luggage bags crowded the backseat of a minivan. But Rose hesitated. The gas station roof kept the premises too well lit. If they tried anything here, she feared they'd be caught.

"Is there anyone in Phoenix you're trying to get back to?" Rose said, trying to distract herself from the fear swirling in her chest.

"What? Like a guy?"

"Anyone that could help us?"

"I haven't spoken to anyone from Phoenix in I don't know how long." Claudia shook her head, blowing out smoke side to side. "What about you? You just got here. Bet you have a lot of friends."

"Just my sister."

She'd only told Claudia about her sister's visit in terms of the backpack full of clothes, food and soap she'd brought. She never spoke about the money out of fear Claudia would rely on Jessica to bring them more.

"No guys?" Claudia said.

Rose blushed. "I haven't dated in years."

"So I was right about that cherry—"

"I'm focusing on my career." She locked eyes with Claudia. "If I met a guy as driven as me, of course I'd date him. That just never happened."

Claudia danced her fingers down Rose's leg. "Maybe you're not looking for a guy."

"Okay," Rose said, putting up her hand, "just because we share the same bed, does not make me gay."

"Doesn't surprise me you never met a dude." Claudia slapped Rose's leg. "You couldn't find a coyote in a border town."

Before Rose could think of any comeback, a brown sedan pulled up to the parking space in front of them. A middle-aged man wearing a t-shirt and shorts stepped out of the car and dropped coins into the air and water machine. A DSLR camera hung around his shoulder.

Rose nudged Claudia and pointed toward the camera.

"How much you think that's worth?" Claudia said.

"700," Rose said, remembering the camera ICE confiscated from her and never returned. "3,000, maybe, depending on the model."

"Pesos?"

"Dollars."

Claudia put out her cigarette. "Remember the plan."

As Rose stood up, a boy in the sedan's backseat caught her eye. He looked no older than seven and battled two action figures in his hands.

"Wait." Rose grabbed Claudia's arm. "There's too much light here, let's go somewhere else."

"That camera alone could pay for the coyote." Claudia pulled Rose to her feet and put a hand on each of her shoulders. "If we don't do this, we'll be stuck here after the shelters expire."

Claudia dug her hands into her pockets and marched toward the man putting air in his tires. Rose followed. This theft would humiliate him in front of his son. But it was only a camera, she thought, he could afford another. If they didn't steal it, she risked her own life. One day, she'd find a way to make this right. She'd start a foundation, become a philanthropist, give more than she ever took. For now, she could only follow Claudia to the sedan.

"Pendejo," Claudia said. She flicked open a butterfly knife and shouted for the man to get on his feet.

"Tome lo que quiera"—the man jumped up, the air hose reeled back into the machine—"no nos haga daño."

Rose pulled the camera strap over the man's head. She'd never stolen anything in her life. She didn't even reach into a friend's refrigerator without asking first. She tried not to look at the boy inside the car.

"Tu cartera," Claudia said, pointing at the man's pants with her knife.

He handed his wallet to Claudia, who threw it to Rose. She almost dropped the wallet, scrambling to grab the pesos as they fell to the ground.

Claudia pointed to the man's wedding band. "Y tu anillo."

Inside the car, the boy covered his head with the action figures, distracting Rose. He appeared terrified, frozen in his seat. If she'd seen her own dad get robbed, she would've felt the same. She only wanted to step inside the car, hug the boy, tell him everything would be okay.

"¡Vámonos!" Claudia said. The man hesitated and Rose understood. The camera and money were replaceable, the ring was not. They'd make more off the ring than the other two items combined, but she couldn't rob him of something so special.

She pointed past the man's head into the dark road beyond the station. "Police!"

"What?" Claudia took her eyes off the man. "Where?"

"Right there. Let's go!"

The man lunged for Claudia's arm. He pried the knife out of her hands and sunk his fingernails into her skin. Rose kicked him in the back of the leg, grabbed Claudia's hand, and sprinted down the street. She felt no fear. Her powerful track legs would help her escape. To keep moving, she dragged Claudia. They ran two blocks before hiding in an alley to catch their breath. Rose peeked back into the street and saw the man hadn't left the gas station. He sat inside the car with his son.

§

Rose sat on her cot in the Nazareth House watching Claudia place what little belongings she had left into her backpack. She packed a change of clothes, a toothbrush, a picture of her mother encased in a locket and a plastic bag filled with chilies. As a repeat deportee, Claudia had long overstayed her welcome. The sisters had asked her to leave to make room for new people. Today was July 10th. Rose had lived in Nogales now for two weeks.

Over Claudia's shoulder, Sister Mercedez stood in the doorway with a girl Rose had never met. The girl glanced at Claudia's bed like a patient cat waiting to be let inside. She looked young and petite, no older than Jessica, yet here she was beginning her own stay in the Nazareth House. Rose thought back to her first night in a shelter, how innocent and scared she felt, how she only wanted to stay safe and find a way out. Now she'd committed robbery, but pawning the camera had given them enough money to leave with the coyote tomorrow.

Sister Mercedez glanced at Rose, causing her to look at the floor. She imagined the nun only had to see her eyes to know she'd robbed a man and his son. Too ashamed, she waited for Mercedez to show the girl another part of the house before she looked up.

"Almost ready?" Rose said, reaching an arm through her backpack strap.

Claudia took a last look at the ceiling. "Let's never come back here."

They slipped on their backpacks, left the bedroom, and stepped outside without ever seeing Sister Mercedez again.

§

With the little change they had to spare, Rose and Claudia stocked up on supplies at a supermarket. The inside of the market was as massive as a warehouse. They pushed a cart down the aisles placing plastic gallons of water, fruit, energy bars and *cajeta*—a spread Claudia called a substitute for peanut butter—inside. Rose splurged on beef jerky, believing the meat would keep up their strength. She tried not to think that they might be purchasing their last meals.

After they loaded their cart, they stood beside each other in the open doorways of the freezer aisle to enjoy the chilled air.

"I think I'll work at a supermarket when we get home," Rose said. "Does that sound like something the whitest girl you know would do?"

Claudia kept her eyes closed. "Not until you brought it up, Rosa."

Rose laughed. The more Claudia called her by her birth name, the more it felt like a term of endearment.

"You think this is enough?" Rose nodded back to the cart. "What if it takes more than three days to cross?"

"The human body needs a gallon of water for every six miles in the desert. We could never carry enough."

"How many miles to the highway?"

"Ask the coyote. I've never gone through Cochise before."

As the cold washed over her, the moment felt so temporary. Soon she'd shut the freezer door, pay for her groceries, and step back outside into the heat. By tomorrow, the very concept of cold would be a distant memory. Again, she felt compelled to ask Claudia about her failed attempts and what new problems they'd face.

Claudia shut the freezer door and pushed the cart forward. Rose walked beside her, feeling the cold air escape from her pores. "Did you ever see anyone die out there?" Rose said. Claudia stared ahead with her mouth closed. "Claudia, I need you to be honest—"

"No, I haven't." Claudia pushed the cart ahead, returning to the water aisle. "We can fit two more gallons in our backpacks. Extra weight's gone after the first day anyways."

Claudia's avoidance proved to Rose she was lying. But calling her out wouldn't do any good. She followed behind Claudia, searching for a way to ask later.

§

Rose and Claudia stood on the concrete hill outside the San Juan Bosco shelter. The man who guarded the door inspected Rose's deportation papers and waved her through, but when he looked at Claudia's papers, he turned her away. Rose wanted to challenge him, but from the regretful way the man looked at her, it was clear neither of them could do anything to change his mind. She didn't want to spend hours hunting for shelters, but refused to let Claudia face the night alone. She exited San Juan Bosco and followed Claudia down the hill.

"You don't have to this," Claudia said as Rose caught up to her. "You still have another night."

Rose didn't need to argue. They tried five more shelters. While each accepted Rose, they turned Claudia away. None had room for a girl who had outlasted her welcome. They tried going back to the Nazareth House, but the door was shut and nobody answered their knocking this late. Without a watch, they had no idea how long they spent searching for shelter. They couldn't exhaust themselves by walking around the city any longer.

With no other option, they decided to sleep in the cemetery. Coming back here made Rose's skin prickle with anxiety. She told herself she was a different person now. She'd matured in two weeks, gained street smarts, she only needed to sleep here one more night. By the time the sun rose, Sol would be waiting for them on the street below. The crossing now sounded like a relief. They'd be out in the middle of nowhere, hikers on a journey, nothing to harm them except the sun. But what happened to Claudia's first coyote? Every time she passed another migrant sitting by the stairs, she thought she saw his eyes gazing at her, his arms waiting to pounce. She took deep breaths to stay calm. Two weeks ago, he'd been finding people who wanted to cross. He'd be out of the city by now, she thought.

They stepped into Jose M. Chavez's plot and sat against the steel gate that surrounded his grave. Claudia lit a cigarette. Her first puff made the tip glow bright like a campfire. Rose imagined the whole cemetery could see them. She would've told Claudia to put it out if she didn't hope the nicotine relaxed her.

Claudia offered her a drag, but she shook her head. "We could die in that desert and you're worried about cancer," Claudia said.

"So you did see someone die." Claudia didn't say anything. Rose scooted closer. "I need you to be real with me right now. Is there anything you're not telling me?"

"I already told you."

"I've known you for two weeks. You have no filter. I don't understand why you won't talk about this—"

"A cousin came with me when I left Tuxtla. He was a year younger than me, he wanted to make money and send it home too. When we got to Altar we hired a coyote..." Claudia paused. Her lips moved but no words came out. Rose nodded, trying to keep up with this new part of Claudia's life. "Our third day in the desert, border patrol raided our party. They arrested me, but my cousin got away. He ran off into the mountains. Nobody ever saw him again." She looked north, though houses and telephone poles blocked any view of the border. "He might not even be dead. He's just wandering around out there, climbing mountains, trying to find a way out. Every time I cross I hope I'll find him. So to answer your question: no, I've never seen anyone die in the desert. But I've seen them disappear. And that's worse than death, because I still have hope when I know I should mourn."

Rose's heart ached because she could relate to Claudia's pain. She rested her head on Claudia's shoulder. "All the time I was in Eloy, I never knew if ICE got to my parents too. I didn't find out they were deported till I got deported. Every day we were in El Comedor, I hoped I'd see them there. I hoped I'd get to eat with them, go back to the shelter with them, make sure they were all right. It took me fifty-three days from the time of my arrest to find them. All that time I never dared think to start mourning."

"You found them in Nogales?"

Rose shook her head. "They're in Caborca."

Claudia pushed Rose off her. "Why aren't you going to Caborca?"

"It's controlled by the cartel—"

"Who gives a shit? You think I'd be going through the desert if I had a ma to go back to?"

"You have family in Tuxtla."

"Them? They think I'm too lazy and stupid to ever make it." She stubbed her cigarette out in the dirt and hid it inside her backpack. "No way, they think I let their son die. They hate me."

"They really said that? Or are you just telling me this 'cause you don't want me to cross?"

"Of course I want you to cross." The moonlight illuminated tears Rose hadn't noticed. "You think I want to be out there with a bunch of dudes I don't know? But if something happens to me, who cares? You got a family here. You don't need to cross."

"I have a sister in Tucson. She needs me."

Claudia stood up. "I need you, your sister needs you…think about yourself."

Rose sat on her knees. "I am thinking about myself. If I go to Caborca the cartel will kill me."

"But you don't know that. You want me to be real with you? The second you set foot in that desert, you're gonna see how little America still feels like home. And even if you get to Tucson you're still gonna be a fucking illegal alien."

"This is my decision," Rose said. Claudia shook her head. She unhooked the gate latch to leave the plot. "Where are you going?"

Claudia sat on the ground outside the gate with her back turned to Rose. She ate from a bag of chilies in her backpack and didn't speak. Rose threw herself on her back, trying to settle her pulse. She looked up at the stars. The Big Dipper and Orion's Belt twinkled above her, same as in Tucson. They made her feel not so far from home.

§

With the first hint of daylight brightening the sky, Rose and Claudia waited on Calle Reforma at the cemetery entrance. She leaned against the bent-open gate and Claudia squatted below her. Neither of them had spoken since last night. If she'd slept more than a couple hours, she didn't think Claudia would've woken her to go down the hill. The familiar grime of lying in the dirt coated her skin. The bags under her eyes felt as heavy as Claudia's looked. Every few minutes, men arrived to loiter near them. The men wore hats, jeans, and long sleeves. They carried backpacks filled to the breaking point and gallon water bottles. Some had thick moustaches, others looked as young as the kids from Amistad Cristiana. Rose thought to introduce herself, she'd be spending the next few days crossing the border with them, but she feared her language barrier would make her sound stupid.

By the time the heat sifted into the Nogales air, a white pick-up truck drove down the street and parked at the entrance. The truck looked like it had withstood every natural element. Rocks had pummeled tiny dents into the grill. Peeled paint flapped in the wind. The front tires looked low on air. Through the frosted windshield, Sol sat beside an obese driver who had pit stains that traveled down his shirtsleeves.

He opened his passenger door and jumped onto the ground. "O.K., amigos." He waved them to the back of the truck. "Vámonos."

Rose, Claudia and five other men walked to the back of the truck. Smog sputtered out of the exhaust pipe. The running engine made the air smell like gasoline.

Sol lowered the tailgate and climbed onboard the bed. A bundle of camping backpacks lay in the truck behind him—no doubt packed with drugs. One at a time, he took the men's money and gave them his hand to climb up. Claudia walked forward, but Rose stood still. The bed of the truck looked like a seat on the world's deadliest rollercoaster. Once he shut the tailgate, there'd be no way out. She thought of the dead man they saw on this very street and imagined her own face being covered by a ratty blanket.

If she trusted Sol, she might be dead in three days. If she walked away, she'd be stuck in Mexico for ten years. With her fate in the shape of a truck bed, ten years didn't sound so long anymore. Her life in Tucson didn't wait perfectly preserved for her. She'd have to live in hiding with her sister and avoid anyone who'd learned the truth about her identity. If border patrol caught her in the desert first, they'd arrest her and send her back to Eloy. She'd need to start all over again, but this time she'd have a felony on her record, a lifetime ban from ever becoming a legal American, and no chance of a political career.

That was another dream she needed to let go. She'd never wanted to be anything except a senator. But from the moment her parents confessed her status, she should've realized that something much larger than a desert separated her from her ambitions. Her goal to become a politician was as unattainable as changing the past. She had to let go of what her life would be, and now start over.

"Claudia, wait." She grabbed Claudia's arm before her friend handed Sol the money. "We don't have to do this. Come to Caborca with me. You could have a family there. My family could be your family."

Claudia's arm went limp. "Now you want to bail?"

"We don't need to do this. Come with me."

Rose held tight to Claudia's hands. She believed this was exactly what Claudia wanted. Nothing waited for her in Phoenix and she already failed at the crossing more times than anyone should. Why wouldn't she want to come with Rose?

Claudia's hands slipped away. "I have to go," she said and she walked to Sol.

Rose's mind raced to think of a way to convince Claudia to stay. Claudia had been determined to cross for so long she needed more than a last minute whim to make her stop, Rose knew that, but why keep going forward with this suicide mission when a new home now opened its doors?

"What if you die?" Rose followed behind her. Claudia paid Sol. "Your mother would never want you to risk your life."

Claudia took Sol's hand and boarded the truck. He motioned for Rose to step forward, but she ignored him. She wished she knew something else to say, to do, that would keep Claudia from leaving. Sol checked his watch, shook his head at her, and jumped off the truck to close the tailgate. The snap of the latch catching sounded as violent as the gunshots Rose heard the night she became friends with

Claudia. Claudia looked so vulnerable that night, so lonely. She hated the idea of her going on alone.

Sol stepped into the passenger seat. The truck drove in reverse, but Rose stepped in its path. The driver honked at her. He stuck his hand out the window and shouted, "Órale." But Rose stood her ground. She tried to make eye contact with Claudia, make her realize how important it was she change her mind.

"I need you," Rose said. "Don't leave." It was the only thing she could do, short of dragging her friend off the truck.

Claudia kept her eyes on her shoes. The truck circled around Rose and took off west on Calle Reforma, where it curved onto Internacional Street and vanished.

The street went quiet again. Only the faint hum of storefronts opening for business came from the city. Rose realized she had no way to contact Claudia. She might never know whether her friend made it to Phoenix, got deported or died.

§

Rose sat on a bus that drove south on Highway 15. Through the clear glass windows, she watched Nogales pass below her. The city looked so innocent from this height. What could be dangerous about a street lined with convenience stores or an intersection with a lawyer's office on the corner? In the lane beside the bus, she noticed a family of four in a sedan. Though the roof obscured their faces, she could tell a man drove the car with his teenage daughter in the backseat. Their hand gestures showed they were having a conversation. When the girl leaned forward to laugh, joy swept through Rose's heart at the thought of her own family.

Tonight, she'd arrive on their doorstep. She'd hold them close. She'd be with them again.

The last time she saw Tucson, she barely blinked as the city faded from view. But she didn't want to look at Nogales anymore. She leaned her head against the window and closed her eyes. Though she never slept, she began to create a new dream.

Eric Z. Weintraub is a Los Angeles native and USC graduate. In addition to writing fiction, he shoots and produces the Telly Award winning foster youth web-series The Storyboard Project. *Dreams of an American Exile* is his first book. For more see EricZWeintraub.com.

Kimberly Sadler is a native of Venice, California. After completing her degree in English from the University of California, Santa Barbara, she wrote for the Arts and Entertainment section of The Independent. Kimberly currently works as an Editor/Writer at the J. Paul Getty Trust and is editor-in-chief of The Getty magazine as well as the monthly e-newsletter.

Ryan Sanchez is an artist, illustrator, and educator who resides in Savannah, GA with his lovely wife Heidi, their beautiful daughter Paloma, and their English bulldog Abbey. He is a professor of illustration at the Savannah College of Art and Design. His illustrations have been widely used in the editorial, advertising, and publishing world and have been recognized by Communication Arts, 3 X 3 Magazine, American Illustration, and the Society of Illustrators. His paintings have been shown in galleries in New York, Los Angeles, San Francisco, Chicago, Seattle, Portland, London, Canada, and Switzerland. In addition, he is also the co-founder and creative director of Spinning Yarn, an illustration agency that represents national and international artist, illustrators, and designers. A better part of his day is spent Photoshopping, painting, picking, poking, posturing, pointing, prognosticating, panicking, pinching, and plotting. For more see ryansanchez.com and spinningyarnreps.com or twitter and Instagram: @rysanz

Made in the USA
San Bernardino, CA
06 January 2019